Murder at the Grey's Hound Mansion

by Maxine Holmgren

Baker's Plays
7611 Sunset Blvd.
Los Angeles, CA 90042
bakersplays.com

MURDER AT THE GREY'S HOUND MANSION was presented by the Sun City Players Club on November 1 and 2, 2008 at Webb Hall in Sun City, California. The production was directed by Betty Jo Adney and C. Susan Carreiro with the following cast:

PHYLLIS. . . . . Carolyn Wilday

COUSIN EARLENE. . . . . .Maxine Holmgren

BEA . . . . Faye Hartline

WILL . . . . Richard Turner

ANNA . . . . C. Susan Carreiro

VICTORIA . . . . Marje Chase

CAINE NINE . . . . Roberto Carrillo

OFFICER OSSIFER. . . . . Sam Alvo

CAST OF CHARACTERS

PHYLLIS – Private Secretary to the late Earl Grey of Hound Mansion. A middle-aged woman, who wears red shoes.

COUSIN EARLENE – Cousin to the late Earl Grey. She is as eccentric as he was. A graduate of an interior decorating correspondence course, she wants to decorate the mansion in shabby chic. She has a habit of mixing metaphors.

BEA – An arthritic, grey haired housekeeper and cook.

WILL – A middle age man, in good physical shape. He was Earl's personal trainer. He is dressed in sweat pants and sweat shirt.

ANNA – A pleasant woman, professional in appearance. She is a dog trainer and has competed and lost in dog shows to the deceased Earl.

VICTORIA – A not too bright eccentric socialite who had her sights set on the Earl and his money.

CAINE NINE – A dog trainer who worked for Earl. Loves dogs. (NOTE: Role can be played by a female with name changed to Kay Nine)

OFFICER OCCIFER – A detective.

(SETTING: Interior of Grey's Hound Mansion. Furnished in formal manner with dark, heavy furniture. Window with dark drapes, pictures of dogs, hunting scenes and trophies complete set.)

*(AT RISE: **PHYLLIS** sits at a large desk, going through papers. Sound of rain and thunder. Doorbell rings.)*

PHYLLIS. *(goes to door)* At last someone has made it through this terrible storm for the reading of the will.

COUSIN EARLENE. *(enters in big flurry. Shakes umbrella, takes off rain coat, puts down shopping bags.)* Hurry, let me in. It never pours, but what it rains! I'm getting soaked and I don't want my fabric samples to get ruined.

BEA. *(slowly shuffles in from kitchen)*

PHYLLIS. *(as she takes coat and tosses it to **BEA**)* Do something with this, will you Bea? Hello, Cousin Earlene.

COUSIN EARLENE. Where is everyone?

PHYLLIS. You're the first to arrive, but I'm certain the rest will be here as soon as they can get through this awful storm. We've all waited a long time for the reading of your cousin Earl's will.

BEA. *(puts coat on coat rack)* Hmph. No one's waited longer than me. I've been waiting forty years for this day.

(sits on chair near coat rack and begins to nod off)

COUSIN EARLENE. You've been keeping house and cooking here at Grey's Hound Mansion for as long as I can remember.

(pulls out bright toss pillows from bag)

This place is so gloomy. But every early cloud gets the worm! I brought some toss pillows to brighten things up. I can't wait to start redecorating! Soon as that attorney gets here and reads the will, no-one will be able to stop me. You'll see!

(places pillows on sofa)

There. Don't you think that looks better?

PHYLLIS. You just can't wait, can you? Earl's been murdered and all you can think about is paisley and brocade! Once the Attorney gets here and reads the will, you might be in for a surprise. Don't count your chintzes before they hatch, if you know what I mean.

COUSIN EARLENE. *(sits on sofa)* Oh, don't be silly. Of course, Earl left Grey's Hound Mansion to me. I'm his only blood relative. And blood is thicker than a duck's back.

PHYLLIS. But you forget, I was his private secretary. His very private secretary. I know everything about him, especially the three F's.

COUSIN EARLENE & BEA. *(together, as **BEA** awakens)* The three F's?

PHYLLIS. Family, friends and finances. I know it all!

(Doorbell rings. Sound of thunder)

PHYLLIS. *(goes to door)* I'll get it. I hope it's the Attorney.

*(**WILL** and **ANNA** enter together. They seem to be arguing, as they take off raincoats, shake umbrellas, etc.)*

WILL. What are you doing here?

ANNA. I have every right to be here. I was invited!

WILL. You've got a lot of nerve, coming here on today of all days.

ANNA. I tell you, I was invited.

WILL. Fat chance.

ANNA. You're one to talk about fat. That's what got you here in the first place.

PHYLLIS. *(takes raincoats, looks for* **BEA,** *hangs them up herself on coat rack)* Stop arguing! Try to have a little respect for the occasion. There will be plenty of time for fighting later. *(to* **ANNA***)* Anna, I think you know the late Earl Grey's Cousin, Cousin Earlene?

ANNA. Yes, hello.

COUSIN EARLENE. Nice to see you again. Here's my card, in case you ever want to decorate your kennels. I specialize in houndstooth check you know.

(Hands her a business card. **ANNA** *sits on chair next to sofa,* **EARLENE** *returns to sofa.)*

PHYLLIS. And this is Bea, she's been the housekeeper here for 40 years.

(nudges **BEA***)*

ANNA. How do you do?

BEA. *(startled as she awakens)* She wants forty beers?

PHYLLIS. *(explaining to others)* She's old and lost her hearing.

(to **BEA***)*

Go back to sleep. Better yet, why don't you fix us some lunch while we're waiting for the Attorney and the others.

*(***BEA** *goes to kitchen, grumbling.)*

WILL. Others? How many are coming anyway? I thought this was a private reading of the will. I came straight from the gym. If I'd known there were going to be outsiders, I'd have changed clothes first.

(sits in chair)

PHYLLIS. I'm the only one who knows who was invited. I know everything.

(Doorbell rings and **VICTORIA** *enters all aflutter. Shakes off raincoat, umbrella, etc.)*

Oh, let me in. It's so frightening out there. The rain, and that terrible thunder. I'm afraid of thunder. And bugs. And heights. And –

PHYLLIS. *(goes to meet her at door and takes raincoat, hangs on coat rack.)* Yes, Victoria, I know. You're afraid of everything.

VICTORIA. And now, murder! To think that Earl was murdered right here. Or there. *(pointing outside)* Or there *(pointing to kitchen)* Oh dear, I don't know where he was murdered. Or how. It's so mysterious!

PHYLLIS. Calm down, Victoria. I know you know everyone here, because I know everything.

VICTORIA. *(startled)* Oh! I thought I would be the only one to inherit – I mean, as Earl's only one true love, I'm sure he left the bulk of his estate to me, so I hope the rest of you won't be too disappointed. *(Sits on sofa, next to* **EARLENE.** *)*

BEA. *(enters from kitchen with tray filled with sandwiches, tea, etc.)* This is the last food I'm ever going to prepare in that kitchen. After the reading of the will, I'm out of here! I've had my fill of fixing fancy dishes for that crazy old man, and his hounds! I'm tired of cooking – in fact, I'm just plain tired.

WILL. I always told you, Bea, your cooking is for the dogs!

(laughs)

BEA. It was bad enough fixing crème brulees, melon custard tarts and fancy French dishes for Earl , but then I had to fix special recipes that Caine Nine gave me for the dogs. Hound Hash, Doggie Delights and Spaniel Smoothies.

PHYLLIS. I'm afraid Bea feels overworked and unappreciated. She really did take good care of Earl, cooking his favorite dishes every day.

BEA. *(as she passes food and tea around then puts tray on coffee table)* Enjoy this food, cause it's the last of my cooking! Once that Attorney reads the will, and I get what Earl promised me, I'll be on my way to Cancun or Bermuda.

VICTORIA. Bermuda! That's where I wanted Earl to take me on our honeymoon. We were talking marriage you know. At least I was. And he was objecting less and less. I knew it was just a matter of time, and I'd wear him down. But I think Will wore him down first. Him and his workout routines. I think he killed him. He had Earl doing so many push-ups his poor old heart couldn't take it. Now he's pushing up daisies!

BEA. As soon as that will is read, I'm collecting my money and I'm going to go on a cruise and let someone else fix exotic fancy dishes for me.

WILL. I kept telling Earl he shouldn't eat the food you prepared for him. All those greasy foods, swimming in rich gravies and sauces. They were enough to clog arteries from here to Chicago. Don't tell me you're sorry he's dead. I think you were trying to hurry up the process.

BEA. Oh, don't look at me like that! Do you really think I had something to do with his death? Sure, I had plenty of opportunity to poison him, but I didn't. I never let the box of rat poison that sat on the shelf above the stove drop into the tea I made for him every night. Even though I was dog-tired myself, I always fixed his nightly cup of tea with special care.

COUSIN EARLENE. Oh, Bea, I'm sure no one suspects you. Does anyone know how Earl died? I've been too busy planning the renovation of the mansion to be bothered with details like that. Don't you think a display of Indian baskets would be nice in the marble foyer?

CAINE NINE. *(Enters from kitchen. Sound of dogs barking. Wears rain boots and poncho. Removes poncho, tosses on chair.)* Hello everyone. I came in the back door so I wouldn't have to walk all around the mansion in the rain. I left a couple of the dogs on the back porch. Hope you don't mind, Bea.

BEA. As long as they don't track mud inside the house, I don't care what you do with them outside. Just keep them out of the kitchen.

PHYLLIS. Do you know everyone here?

CAINE. Well, I seldom leave the kennels, you know. Earl always kept me so busy training the dogs for all the dog shows. Of course, I know Earlene and Bea, but I don't believe I've met the others.

PHYLLIS. This is Caine Nine, Earl's dog trainer. He lives on the estate, and does all the training and grooming of the dogs. He's responsible for all the awards and trophies Earl won.

ANNA. *(as she shakes hands)* Really? I've never seen you at a dog show. My name is Anna.

CAINE. Earl never let me attend. He liked to take all the glory for himself.

WILL. *(rises – shakes hands with **CAINE**)* And I'm Will, I was Earl's personal trainer. It must have been hard to stay in the background and let Earl collect all the accolades.

CAINE. Earl always said he'd make it right for me someday. I guess the day has finally come. When will the will be read?

(shakes hands with **VICTORIA**, *then sits)*

(sound of dogs barking)

VICTORIA. Pleased to meet you. I do wish your dogs would stop barking! They sound ferocious. *(shivers in fear)*

COUSIN EARLENE. *(rises, crosses to* **CAINE***)* Hello. Here's my card. I can help you decorate that little cottage you live in, back of the kennels. Do you like gingham? A penny earned is for a rainy day.

(Phone rings. **PHYLLIS** *goes to desk to answer.* **COUSIN EARLEN** *returns to the sofa.)*

PHYLLIS. Earl Grey's Mansion – Phyllis speaking.
Yes. Oh, dear. Alright. I'll tell them. Thank you for calling. Good Bye.
That was theAttorney. I just knew it would be, because I know everything. The bridge is out, and he has to take a detour. He will be a little late, but it shouldn't be much longer. He'd like us all to wait right here. He said we could entertain ourselves.

(An awkward silence begins.)

*(***PHYLLIS** *drums fingers on desk.)*

*(***VICTORIA** *fidgets and looks around nervously.)*

*(***CAINE** *begins to whistle and pace.)*

*(***BEA** *nods off.)*

*(***WILL** *starts to exercise. [Pushups, knee bends or stretches])*

*(***EARLENE** *goes to window drapes with fabric swatches)*

*(***ANNA** *– twiddles thumbs)*

(thunder)

PHYLLIS. Well, this is awkward! Surely we can converse with one another. Anna, everyone was surprised when you arrived, except me. I knew you were coming, because I know everything. Why don't you explain to them how that argument between you and Earl first got started?

WILL. She probably came to celebrate Earl's death. Everybody knows she hated him.

CAINE. *(to* **ANNA***)* Earl always talked about you. I'm glad I finally get to meet you. He always bragged about his dogs winning over yours at every dog show.

*(***EARLENE** *returns to sofa to hear* **ANNA***'s story.)*

ANNA. No one was more surprised than I when I received the call to attend the reading of the will. At first I thought it was just another of his dirty tricks, but the Attorney assured me it was not. I guess Earl was finally feeling remorseful over the way he cheated me, and was trying to make amends. Reaching out from the grave for my forgiveness, I suppose.

VICTORIA. Oh, don't talk about reaching out from a grave. That sounds so scary!

(shudders, looks around nervously)

ANNA. *(Rises. Paces as she speaks)* It all started a couple of years ago. Earl and I just happened to be attending the same auction for pedigreed pooches. There was a fine looking beagle that Earl and I both were attracted to. I remember he had long drooping ears and soulful deep dark brown eyes. *(pause)* The beagle was nice looking too.

Earl knew I wanted that particular pooch, but he didn't care. He bid better for Bagel the Beagle, beating me by bidding better before I could buy the beagle, Bagel. When the ending bugle blew, my bid was banished. He had bought the beagle Bagle and I was left holding the bag.

CAINE. *(stands)* I remember that beagle! Earl brought him home and I worked with him and trained him. He won several blue ribbons, and the coveted Blue Banner. Did you have an entry in the Blue Banner Kennel Show, too?

ANNA. Of course I did! I bought another Beagle, Bangle. My Bangle was beat by Bagel at every dog show, and I suspected foul play. I think Earl was bribing those judges, but I could never prove anything.

CAINE. But Bagel was better! He won Best of Show, Best of Hound, Best of Howl, Best of Bark – I know, because I trained him. I taught him how to walk down the runway, and howl and bark. I taught him everything I knew, and I know it all.

PHYLLIS. No, I know it all. You may know about dogs, but I know everything else about Earl. I know about his fame and his fortune. Go on with your story, Anna.

(thunder and dogs bark)

CAINE. Excuse me, I'll give the dogs a biscuit or two to quiet them down. Would anyone else care for one?

(CAINE offers handful to others, exits munching on one himself.)

ANNA. It's true. Bangle always lost to Bagel, but not because he was better. He became bitter. Not Bagel, but Bangle. Became bitter. So, I took him to the famous dog psychiatrist, Dr. Bramble. It cost me a bundle, but he didn't bungle the business. After months of treatment, Dr. Bramble pronounced Bangle better! Cured, he said. He was so confident that Bangle had overcome his poor self image that he could be entered in the Best of Beagles Competition in Burbank.

VICTORIA. Victoria – Burbank is so lovely in the springtime. Not like this gloomy place.

(jumps as we hear the sound of thunder again)

ANNA. So I took Bangle to Burbank. It was so exciting. Banners were flying, people were bustling about, and Beagles from all over the world were there to compete. Of course, Bagel was there too. Bangle looked beautiful. His coat was brushed to a glossy shine, his nose was polished and his ears were waxed. He looked great. When the judging began, I just knew this time Bangle would win over Bagel.

COUSIN EARLENE. Hurray! Bangle won. Would you like me to design a room for his award? Maybe something in hunters green or a plaid.

ANNA. Not so fast. That conniving Earl bribed the judges. This time I saw it. I saw him slip an envelope to one of the judges. Of course, he denied it. But once again, Bangle was defeated by Bagel. Defeated once again by Earl Grey and his hound.

(sits)

VICTORIA. Poor Bangle. But that doesn't mean Earl left you any money in his will. I'm sure he left it all to me, his one true love. I miss him so.

(begins to sob)

WILL. *(to ANNA)* Well, it's pretty plain to see that you're not mourning the death of your competitor.

ANNA. Now Bangle will have a chance of winning the awards and ribbons that should have been his all along.

(BEA *has nodded off again.)*

VICTORIA. I wish the Attorney would get here. Is it still raining so hard?

WILL. Cats and dogs! Look at Bea. She's fallen asleep again. She's useless as a housekeeper. How long has she been around here anyway?

PHYLLIS. Bea, wake up!

(**BEA** *awakens, tries to pay attention.*)

Will was just asking how long you've been house-keeper here at the mansion.

BEA. You want to know if there's deer at the mansion? Is it hunting season already?

PHYLLIS. Turn up your hearing aid! I said Will wants to know how long you've been housekeeper here at the mansion. Of course, I know, because I know everything, but why don't you tell everyone else.

BEA. Oh, it's been a long, long time. Let's see, I was in my forties when I first came here. It seemed like a nice place, even if Earl did let his hounds have the run of the house. I was younger than, I didn't have arthritis, so I could keep up with the cleaning.

COUSIN EARLENE. When I take over the mansion, you won't have to worry about cleaning the Oriental rugs. I'm going to replace them with bamboo mats. That will go nicely with the lace curtains, don't you think?

BEA. (*begins to pace*) Ten years later I developed an allergy to dogs. I sneezed and sneezed, and had trouble breathing, so I wanted to quit and find another job. I thought maybe somewhere on the coast. Ocean air might be good for me. (*Blow nose.*) I told Earl my intentions and he surprised me.

VICTORIA. Oh, Earl was good at surprises. He loved to surprise me too. He'd often hide when he saw me coming down the path on my bicycle. But I always found him. He said he was surprised I never gave up. I do miss him so. Where else will I find someone with a mansion – I mean, manners like he had. You said he surprised you, Bea?

BEA. Yes. He said he didn't want me to leave. In fact, he got real upset about it. He said that if I stayed on, he'd make it right with me, in his will. He promised me a pretty good sized amount, too.

(**BEA** *uses nose spray.*)

VICTORIA. Oh, I hope you don't have anything contagious. I'm afraid of germs.

BEA. About ten years later, I got arthritis so bad in my hips and back, I could hardly get around. I wanted to quit then too, but Earl talked me out of it again. He said he'd double the amount if I stayed on.

VICTORIA. That was before he met me, of course.

BEA. Ten years late I had blood pressure problems. I nearly had a stroke. I told Earl I really had to quit. Then he told me I wouldn't get a dime from his will, unless I was still working for him when he died.

(**BEA** *takes more pills.*)

(**CAINE** *returns and sits.*)

VICTORIA. I'm sure you misunderstood him. He intended to leave everything to me. That's why I stayed engaged. Oh, I know you all think I was after his money, but it was true love, I tell you. I loved everything about him.

PHYLLIS. Yes, you loved his business, his estate, his stocks and bonds, his cars, his boats, his money – everything except him!

(**COUSIN EARLENE** *is busy holding more fabric swatches against the window, trying to decide which one to choose. They are an assortment of bright, gaudy prints.*)

BEA. Well, now he's finally gone, and it's time for me to collect. I've been looking forward to this day for forty years!

(**BEA** *collects plates and exits to kitchen.*)

PHYLLIS. Forty years is a long time. But then, you've know Earl all your life, haven't you Cousin Earlene? You don't seem too saddened by his sudden death, though.

COUSIN EARLENE. Who, me? Well, of course I am just devastated that my rich cousin has finally passed away. But he's in a better place, I'm sure. Anyplace would be better than this gloomy mansion of his. I offered to redecorate it for him, but never would let me. He said I should leave well enough is hard to find – or something like that.

VICTORIA. Oh, you're an interior decorator?

COUSIN EARLENE. Yes, I took a correspondence course from the Home Interior Decorating for Dummies School. I had some lovely chintz curtains picked out for the drawing room, but Earl insisted on leaving those dark brown drapes instead. *(Show swatches.)* He said it was the same color as one of his prize winning hounds. Personally, I thought they looked like they came from the flea market.

VICTORIA. That's funny. Flea market drapes for Hound Mansion.

COUSIN EARLENE. I had great plans for the library, too. I thought some country baskets would be nice out there, instead of those trophies. Of course, they wouldn't go with the marble floor, so that would have to go. He didn't like that idea, but you know what they say. If at first you don't succeed, don't put all your eggs in one basket. I don't know why you'd want to put eggs in the library, but then, I never change horses in the middle of a job worth doing.

CAINE. And I thought Earl was a strange one! It must run in the family.

BEA. *(returns from kitchen)* What'd you say? Your son has a Camry?

PHYLLIS. Nevermind, Bea. Please go on, Earlene

COUSIN EARLENE. Once I overheard him talking about the great Dane, and I got so excited. I thought he's finally taken an interest in Danish modern design. I ran to my room and got my catalogues of Danish modern furniture, but when I showed them to Earl, he laughed at me. He said he was talking about a dog. How was I to know there was a breed of dogs called Great Danes? That's what I get for counting my chickens before I walked a mile in their shoes.

WILL. I bet you didn't like getting laughed at. *(to others)* It might have made her angry enough to kill Earl, so she could do whatever she wanted .

COUSIN EARLENE. Well, who's laughing now, I'd like to know. He can't stop me now. I could paint the whole mansion purple, if I wanted to. Of course, I wouldn't do that. It wouldn't go with the chartreuse striped wall paper I've ordered for the library. They say actions speak louder than an apple a day, so I'll start ordering Waving Lee fabrics right away.

(sound of thunder and dogs barking)

VICTORIA. Can't you make those dogs be quiet? They scare me, they sound so fierce.

CAINE. *(goes to door and shouts to dogs)* Quiet! Quiet! The storm is making them nervous. I hope the Attorney gets here soon. If he doesn't, I'll take them down to the kennels.

VICTORIA. That's where you belong anyway. I don't know why you're up here with real people. You spend more time with dogs than people.

CAINE. It's true. I love those hound dogs. I work with them, eat with them, talk with them.

VICTORIA. You talk with them? Come now, surely you don't believe they can talk to you?

CAINE. Of course I do. You've probably heard of the horse whisperer? Well, I'm the hound whisperer. I'd be as famous as that horse whisperer, if it wasn't for Earl. Hollywood would have made a movie about me, but Earl wouldn't let anyone know about me. He kept me in the background, unknown and unloved except by the hounds.

VICTORIA. That must have made you pretty angry.

CAINE. I was the one that taught those hounds everything they knew. I was the one that taught Hillary the Hound how to howl with her ears pointed straight up. It wasn't easy, let me tell you. It should sound like this *(demonstrates by howling)*

VICTORIA. Oh, that sounds so mournful. Did you teach them to talk with you, too?

CAINE. Well, they were barking fairly well, but they weren't barking in complete sentences. I had to teach them how to do that. Of course, you all know that hounds communicate with each other by barking, don't you? Oh yes, they have a language all their own. For instance, "Hello" sounds like this. *(barks once)* And "how are you" sounds like "Rrruf rruf rruff!" But I don't want to give all my secrets away.

WILL. *(to others)* He's as nutty as that cousin with the curtains.

CAINE. There was a time when a reporter from the New York Daily Beagle, I mean Bugle wanted to interview me. Somehow they heard about me, and wanted to do a big story about me, with pictures and everything. I would have been famous! But Earl was so jealous he turned the Rottweilers out on that poor reporter and he never came back. My one chance at fame was gone – because of Earl's jealousy. But he promised to make it up to me in his will. And that's why I'm here, for the reading of the will.

WILL. It's plain to see you're glad Earl is dead. Now you can collect all the trophies and awards and such yourself.

CAINE. Yes, I'll be famous at last. But if you think I killed Earl, you're all barking up the wrong tree! I'm sure you're anxious to hear the will read, too, Will. Didn't he promise to leave you an inheritance?

PHYLLIS. Yes, I know he promised that to you, Will. I know everything. And I know about those little accidents that kept happening down at the gym.

WILL. You mean the time the sun lamp fell into the pool? I tripped, I tell you. I tripped over the extension cord, and accidentally knocked the sun lamp into the pool. How did I know Earl could move so fast? I mean, it was a good thing he could move that fast and get out of the pool before the lamp hit the water. My goodness, that could have been a tragic accident.

COUSIN EARLENE. Yes, that was a very expensive sun lamp, and it would have been ruined.

PHYLLIS. And the time he flew off the tread mill? I suppose that was an accident, too?

WILL. Well, you know how unreliable machines can be. Earl was doing quite well on the treadmill. He would plod along at a slow pace. He couldn't go very fast, because of his heart, you know. I was right by his side, encouraging him. I noticed a little dust on the control panel, and was just cleaning the machine, when it malfunctioned and went into high speed. Earl was thrown right off, clear across the room. I thought for sure he was a goner, but he was stronger than he looked. He survived that, too.

PHYLLIS. And then there was that incident with the barbells. I know about that because –

EVERYONE. You know everything!

WILL. Oh, that little incident. *(laughs)* It was nothing, really. I added weight lifting to Earl's workout schedule. Nothing too heavy of course, because of his bad heart. I had the dumb-bell, I mean I had him lifting dumbbells to start with, just light ones. Then I noticed he was actually getting stronger. So I increased the weights to 75, then 80 then 150. I wondered how much longer he could last, er- uh – how much longer he could blast away on those barbells. But he continued to do well, and I continued to wait – I mean continued with the weights.

(door bell)

PHYLLIS. *(going to door)* Do come in. You must be Attorney Jones?

OFFICER. *(takes off coat and shows badge)* Allow me to introduce myself. I am Officer Occifer, I work in the Homicide Department.

VICTORIA. A detective! *(VICTORIA rises.)*

WILL. What are you doing here? Where's the Attorney?

OFFICER. The Attorney won't be coming. That was just a ruse to get you all here. You see, we now know who killed Earl of Grey's Hound Mansion. It was one of you!

VICTORIA. Oh! I think I'm going to faint! *(falls to chair and fans herself)*

CAINE. You mean, the killer is one of us?

OFFICER. Exactly!

COUSIN EARLENE. I knew it was you! *(points to WILL)*

BEA. I knew it was you *(points to ANNA)*

ANNA. I knew it was you *(points to VICTORIA)*

VICTORIA. I knew it was you *(points to BEA)*

CAINE. I knew it was you *(points to PHYLLIS)*

WILL. I knew it was you *(points to CAINE)*

PHYLLIS. I knew it was one of you. I know everything!

OFFICER. Earl was strangled with a silk scarf. And in the corner we found the initials of *(dramatic pause)* E.M.G.

*(**EARLENE** tries to think who that might be.)*

PHYLLIS. Cousin Earlene Mae Grey! You killed Earl! Your own cousin!

BEA. Just couldn't wait to get your hands on the mansion, could you!

WILL. I knew you had a mean streak in you, you greedy lunatic!

COUSIN EARLENE. *(rises and goes to* **OFFICER***)* No, wait. You don't understand! It's true. Those are my initials. But I embroidered them on *all* the silk scarves I made as Christmas gifts for everyone last year. I gave everyone a silk scarf, and I signed each one with my initials E.M.G. But each person received a different color. And I didn't make a scarf for myself. I was going to, but you know how it is, a stitch in time gets the last laugh. I had to shop for all my other cousins and –

PHYLLIS. That's true! She gave me a red scarf and her initals were embroidered in the corner.

BEA. She gave me a grey scarf.

OFFICER. Do you remember who got what, I mean, to whom got which, I mean to whom you gave what color scarf?

COUSIN EARLENE. Well, let me think. Phyllis, red – to match her shoes, Bea, grey – to match her hair, – what color was the scarf that was used as the murder weapon?

OFFICER. It was green! With a purple border! Who did you give that color to? That person is the murderer!

VICTORIA. Oh, the suspense! I'm terrified!

COUSIN EARLENE. I remember perfectly who I gave it to. It matched their jacket. I gave it to – *(dramatic pause)* Will!

WILL. *(pulls gun)* Stay back! You've ruined it all! Now I'll never inherit that money. It's true, I got tired of waiting for Earl to kick the bucket. I faked those accidents, trying to kill him off, but the old coot wouldn't cooperate. I finally lost patience and told him I was going to teach him karate. I threw him to the floor and then I showed him my special scarf choke hold. Ha, ha – guess I showed it to him a little too long. But you won't get me.

OFFICER. Drop that gun. You'll never get away. There are other Occifers, I mean officers right at the front door.

WILL. Then I guess I'll have to use the back door.

> (WILL *makes his escape out the back door, waving gun at everyone.*)

Stay back, I'm warning you, or I'll shoot!

(sound of dogs barking and growling)

(VICTORIA *faints – all rush to her, except for* OFFICER.*)

(There are excited exclamations from all as they try to revive her.)

OFFICER. *(goes to window.)* He's getting away! *(pause)* Oh, look!

(All go to window and look out above café curtain. Audience does not see what is going on outside window, but a dummy, dressed like Will could be seen above café curtain, tossed in air. Sound of dogs barking and growling grows louder. Excited exclamations come from all.)

VICTORIA. *(sees she is not center of attraction, rouses herself and goes to window also)* What's going on? Oh, my goodness!

WILL. *(bursts in through same exit door. Clothes are all ripped to shreds and he is covered in mud and blood.)* I surrender! I surrender! Just keep those hounds away from me! They nearly killed me. Take me away! Please! *(holds out hands for hand-cuffs)*

OFFICER. *(puts hand-cuffs on* **WILL** *and reads rights to him as he leads him out front door)* I arrest you for the murder of Earl Grey. You have the right to remain silent; you have the right to have an attorney…

BEA. *(goes center stage)* Look at the mess on the rug. Am I supposed to clean that up? Well, no thank you! I quit! I'm outta here! *(exits)*

VICTORIA. *(center stage)* You mean the Attorney isn't coming at all? There's no reading of the will today? Then I may as well go home and see if any one has responded to the ad I placed on the Internet singles website. *(exits stage right)*

COUSIN EARLENE. *(center stage)* Speaking of silk, I think silk lampshades would be pretty in here. I'll go get my silk swatches. *(exits stage right)*

CAINE. *(center stage)* Well, the guard dogs guarded Earl even after his death. I think I'll give them a big treat. *(exits stage left)*

ANNA. *(center stage)* I might have known it was another trick. Earl never intended to make amends with me. I'm going home. *(exit stage right)*

PHYLLIS. *(center stage)* I knew it would rain today. I knew the Attorney wasn't really coming. I knew there would be no reading of the will. I knew the detective was coming. I knew it all along. Because I know everything! And I know that *(pause)* This is THE END!

(Curtain)

COSTUME PLOT

PHYLLIS. A business suit with red shoes. Wears reading glasses, plain hair style.

COUSIN EARLENE. Very colorful, frilly outfit, complete with large carry-all bag. Wears raincoat, has bright colored umbrella. Bag full of fabric swatches, samples, brochures, etc. Business cards.

BEA. Plain colored skirt and blouse, covered by big, well used apron. Plain walking shoes. Hearing aid.

WILL. Sweat pants and sweat shirt, athletic shoes. Must have matching set of sweat pants and shirt that are torn, mud and blood stained for quick change. Raincoat, umbrella. Gun hidden in clothes.

ANNA. Business Pants suit or jodphurs and jacket. Raincoat, umbrella.

VICTORIA. Fancy outfit, boa, jewelry, etc. Raincoat, umbrella.

CAINE NINE. Jeans, shirt and jacket. Rain poncho.

OFFICER OCCIFER. Black raincoat over business suit. Wallet with badge, police I.D. Handcuffs.

SET PLOT

Interior scene of very formal, dark and forboding living room. Outside door is stage right, kitchen leading to outside back door is stage left. A window is center stage. Pictures, statues of dogs adorn room.

PROPERTY PLOT

STAGE RIGHT: Door to outside, umbrella stand, coat rack nearby. Desk and chair, phone, papers, etc. Extra chair.

CENTER STAGE: Formal sofa, coffee table, chair.

STAGE LEFT: Door to kitchen and outside back door. Chair and end table.

OFFSTAGE TO LEFT: Serving tray, sandwiches, plates, coffee and cups.

NOTE

Will could wear torn up sweat suit under the sweat suit he wears on stage. During commotion of dogs barking and growling ferociously, he could quickly remove outer suit, smear mud/blood on his face and stagger back on stage. Meanwhile, a dummy, dressed like Will, is seen *(through window)* tossed in the air, fighting with dogs.

AUTHOR'S NOTE

Several people wanted to know who finally inherited Earl Grey's fortune, so here is a brief explanation of what happened after the curtain went down.

Bea – Bea inherited a fairly nice sum of money. She went on an ocean cruise, but became terribly sea sick. She gave up cruising and moved to the Arizona Desert instead. In a few months her arthritis disappeared. She took up tennis. The desert air was so good for her that her allergies disappeared. She bought a cat because she was tired of dogs. She was so happy in her new lifestyle, her blood pressure became normal. She opened a tea room specializing in Earl Grey tea, creme brulees, custard tarts and smoothies.

Caine Nine – Without Earl Grey to keep him in the dark, he came out in the open and became famous as the Hound Whisperer. He has his own TV show, talking to dogs and teaching them how to respond in complete sentences. He used the small inheritance he received to develop a line of dog biscuits "Doggie Delights" and sold them through his online website: www.Caineninescanines.com.

Anna – Anna used her small inheritance and bought a better beagle, Banana. He became her best beagle and even beat Bangle. She opened a chain of Beagle Boutiques specializing in Beagle bandanas, booties, brushes, buntings, banners and beautiful books of beagles. She became obsessed with beagles, banishing her brothers bulldogs from the Beagle bistro. Dr. Bramble became her beau and they bred a brood of beagles as a business.

Earlene – Earlene got most of the inheritance. She immediately redecorated the entire mansion as only she could. The Decorating for Dummies school used it as a role model - of what not to do. She is presently installing a moat around the mansion. She intends to tint the water pink, her favorite color, and fill it with green fish hoping to achieve a polka dot effect. She has decorated the front yard with plastic pink flamingos. The neighbors are circulating a petition.

Victoria – Victoria did not inherit anything. Instead, she went online and began relationships with many men, none of whom had mansions. She visited any of them that provided her airfare. This took her to London, Cambodia, Paris, Bangladesh, and Monte Carlo. She was very disappointed to discover the prince in Monte Carlo was a fraud. She has not been seen since she flew to Africa to meet a big game hunter. It is feared she was the big game.

Phyllis – Phyllis received a small inheritance. She got an online degree in counseling and set up shop as the Lady who Knows Everything. For a fee, she answered questions about family, friends and finances. She also gave advice to the lovelorn. This led to an appearance on a popular talk show and then she was set up with her own show "Ask Dr. Phyllis."

Will – After surrendering to Officer Occifer to get away from the dogs, Will overpowered the Officer with a karate chop and ran away. He fled the country, eventually landing in Transylvania working as a physical trainer to a Count. He was very unhappy with the work there, as he was required to work night hours. He suspected something strange about the Count, but Transylvania was such a good place to hide out. He hated to leave, but the bats were getting on his nerves. (He was not named in Earl Grey's will.)

Officer Occifer – Officer Occifer never gave up hunting for Will. He was very remorseful that Will had escaped his grasp and ran away before the other officers took him into custody. He took a special police academy course in "How to Handcuff a Prisoner" and also took up running and became a track star. He was determined to never lose another prisoner again. He was last seen with a ticket to Transylvania in one hand and handcuffs in the other.

* 9 7 8 0 8 7 4 4 0 3 1 6 9 *